THE SECRET ME: MY MIND

A DOUBLEDAY BOOK 978 0 385 61399 6

Published in Great Britain by Doubleday,
an imprint of Random House Children's Books
A Random House Group Company

This edition published 2008

1 3 5 7 9 10 8 6 4 2

Text and illustrations copyright © Random House Children's Books, 2008
Text by Alison Ritchie
Illustrations by Nila Aye
Design by Rachel Clark

RANDOM HOUSE CHILDREN'S BOOKS
61–63 Uxbridge Road, London W5 5SA

www.kidsatrandomhouse.co.uk
www.rbooks.co.uk

Addresses for companies within The Random House Group Limited can be
found at: www.randomhouse.co.uk/offices.htm

THE RANDOM HOUSE GROUP Limited Reg. No. 954009

A CIP catalogue record for this book is available from the British Library.

Printed in China

The Secret Me

My Mind

DOUBLEDAY

Introduction

Does everything sometimes feel all wrong? Are you happy one minute, and tearful or irritable the next? Do those days when life was simple and easy seem a long, long time ago? So what's going on? Hormones, that's what! Chemicals produced in your brain and reproductive organs are zooming around your body, creating emotions that are really difficult to deal with. Everything's changing and you have no control over it, and while your body is getting itself together, you feel like you're falling apart.

Don't worry, you're so normal it's not true! It's the same for everyone. Your body has its own timetable, but sometime between the ages of about seven and eighteen, your body goes through massive changes and your mind goes through the mill with it. No need to panic – there are ways of getting back in control and feeling a whole lot better. The more you learn what to expect, the easier it will be to handle it.

This book offers advice on how to feel good in yourself and about yourself, and how to go through all these changes and still have fun at the same time!

Love Ali
xxx

all about me

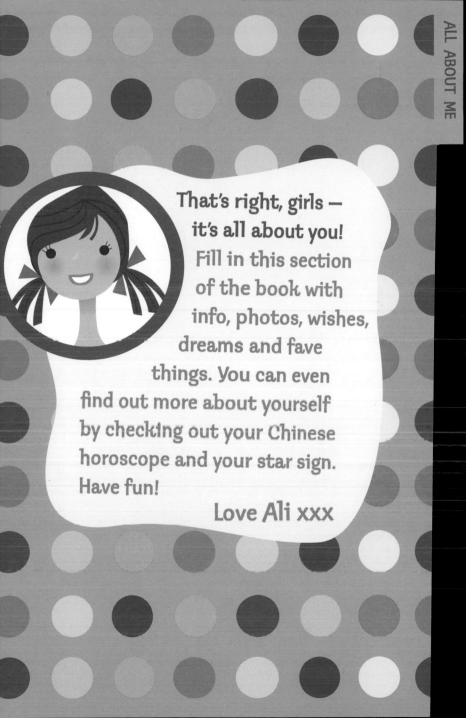

That's right, girls —
it's all about you!
Fill in this section
of the book with
info, photos, wishes,
dreams and fave
things. You can even
find out more about yourself
by checking out your Chinese
horoscope and your star sign.
Have fun!

Love Ali xxx

This Book is the
property of

. . . .

. . . .

IF YOU'RE NOT ME, STOP RIGHT THERE!

If you do find this, please, please, please send it back to me at

This is me!

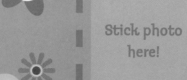

Stick photo here!

My friends call me

....

Age

....

Eye colour

....

Braininess on a scale of 1–10

....

Hair colour

....

Star Quality!

My birthday is on ....

That makes me a gorgeous ....

Fill in your star sign here

Aries – 21 March to 20 April
Energetic Enthusiastic Adventurous

Taurus – 21 April to 21 May
Reliable Gentle Patient

Gemini – 22 May to 22 June
Witty Cheerful Imaginative

Cancer – 23 June to 22 July
Caring Creative Sensitive

Leo – 23 July to 23 August
Generous Daring Intelligent

Virgo — 24 August to 22 September
Kind Hardworking Creative

Libra — 23 September to 23 October
Charming Artistic Independent

Scorpio — 24 October to 22 November
Thoughtful Loyal Shrewd

Sagittarius — 23 November to 21 December
Lucky Talkative Optimistic

Capricorn — 22 December to 20 January
Patient Kind Honest

Aquarius — 21 January to 18 February
Friendly Optimistic Understanding

Pisces — 19 February to 20 March
Unselfish Easy-going Loving

Best Buddies

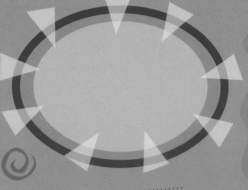

Stick in photos of your best buddies

Name..........................
   Birthday..........................
   Star sign..........................
She is cool because..................
....

Name..........................
   Birthday..........................
   Star sign..........................
She is cool because..................
....

Name..........................
   Birthday..........................
   Star sign..........................
She is cool because..................
....

Name..........................
   Birthday..........................
   Star sign..........................
She is cool because..................
....

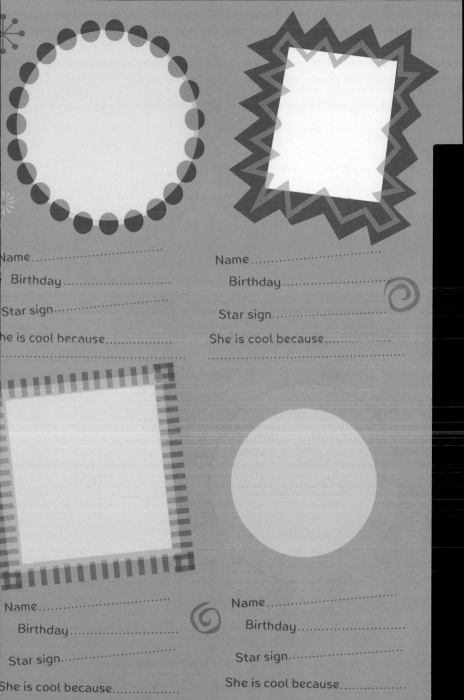

Name.................................

Birthday.............................

Star sign.............................

She is cool because..................

Name.................................

Birthday.............................

Star sign.............................

She is cool because..................

Name.................................

Birthday.............................

Star sign.............................

She is cool because..................

Name.................................

Birthday.............................

Star sign.............................

She is cool because..................

Chinese Horoscopes

I was born in . . . .

That makes me a . . . .

DRAGON

GOAT

TiGER

DOG

MONKEY

SNAKE

OX

CHiCKEN

PiG

HORSE

RABBiT

RAT

TiGER

2010 1998 1986 1974
1962 1950 1938 1926
Popular Talkative
Courageous

OX

2009 1997 1985 197
1961 1949 1937 1925
Steadfast Honoura
Easy-going

RAT
2008 1996 1984 1972
1960 1948 1936 1924
Sociable Ambitious
Cool

GOAT
2003 1991 1979 1967
1955 1943 1931 1919
Generous Artistic
Elegant

PIG
2007 1995 1983 1971
1959 1947 1935 1923
Strong Chivalrous
Home-loving

HORSE
2002 1990 1978 1966
1954 1942 1930 1918
Graceful Cheerful
Passionate

DOG
2006 1994 1982 1970
1958 1946 1934 1922
Loyal Reliable Fair

SNAKE
2001 1989 1977 1965
1953 1941 1929 1917
Wise Extravagant
Determined

CHICKEN
2005 1993 1981 1969
1957 1945 1933 1921
Stylish Eccentric
Inventive

DRAGON
2000 1988 1976 1964
1952 1940 1928 1916
Charming Energetic
Brave

MONKEY
2004 1992 1980 1968
1956 1944 1932 1920
Popular Talkative
Successful

RABBIT
1999 1987 1975 1963
1951 1939 1927 1915
Warm Sensitive
Clever

My Fab Family

Name . . . .

Relation to me . . . .

Born . . . .

Chinese Year of the . . . .

Name . . . .

Relation to me . . . .

Born . . . .

Chinese Year of the
. . . .

Name . . . .   Relation to me . . . .

Born . . . .   Chinese Year of the . . . .

Name . . . .

Relation to me . . . .

Born . . . .

Chinese Year of the . . . .

Stick in photos to make your own family tree

Name . . . .

Relation to me . . . .

Born . . . .

Chinese Year of the . . . .

Name . . . .

Relation to me . . . .

Born . . . .

Chinese Year of the . . . .

Name . . . .

Relation to me . . . .

Born . . . .

Chinese Year of the . . . .

My Favourite Things

1 ....
2 ....
3 ....
4 ....
5 ....

BOUTIQUE

search the web

Stick photo here!

6 ....

7 ....

8 ....

9 ....

10 ....

CELEBRITY
£2.48

EXCLUSIVE
Wedding Pictures

Sample list:

1 Chocolate mousse
2 Reading celeb gossip
3 Clothes shopping
4 My cat
5 My birthday
6 Surprises
7 Hanging out with my mates
8 Dancing ♡
9 Surfing the net
10 Texting

What I'm Like

Circle the words that best describe you. It's OK to shout about yourself because you are utterly WONDERFUL — but remember — be truthful: no one's perfect!

Generous

Sensitive

Friendly

Patient

moody

Loving   Enthusiastic

SeLFiSH

Outgoing   BRAVE

sad   mean

Reliable   Hardworking

insensitive

shy

Creative

Loyal

MESSY

grumpy

Clever

FUNNY

Positive

STROPPY

Honest

kind

HAPPY

Thoughtful

Tidy

ENERGETIC

My mates say I'm..

....

....

....

My Hopes and Dreams

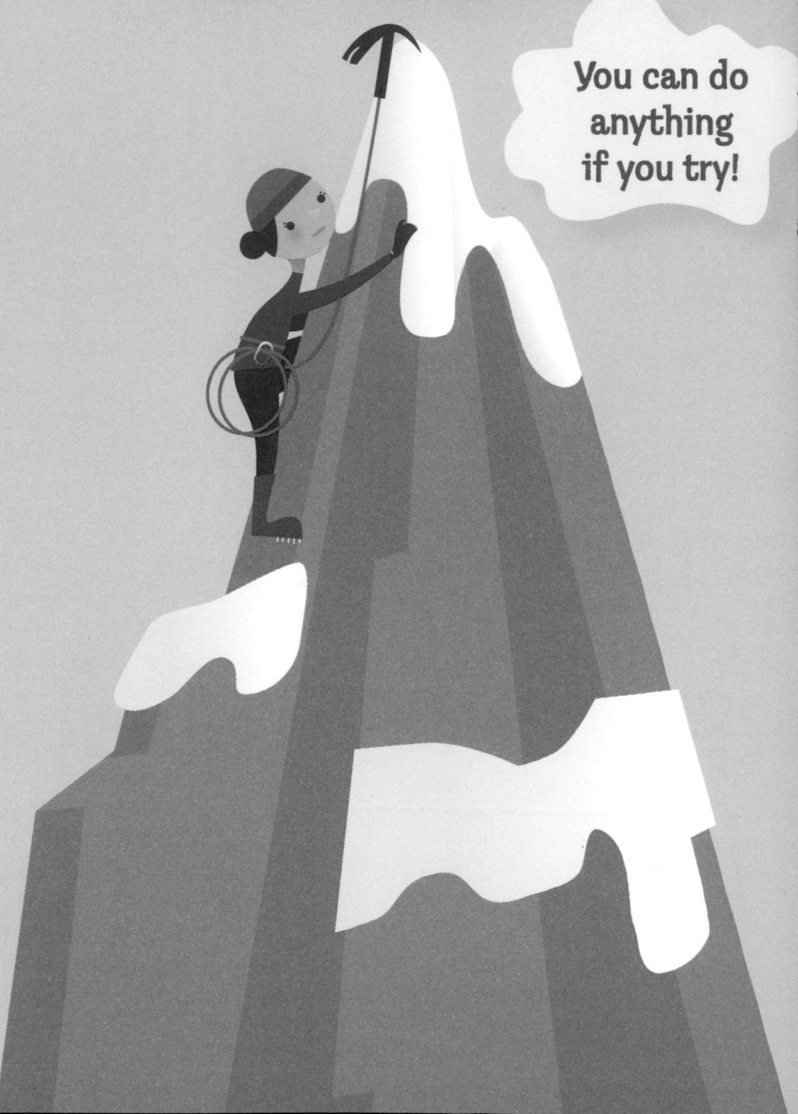

What do you want out of life?

Where will you travel? What job will you do? What kind of house will you live in? Will you have pets? What will your boyfriend look like? The world is your oyster, so get out there, girl!

Can't Do Without

What I'd take to a desert island and why!

1

2

3

4

5

6

Ten Top Tens

FiLMS
1
2
3
4
5
6
7
8
9
10

BOOKS
1
2
3
4
5
6
7
8
9
10

PLACES
1
2
3
4
5
6
7
8
9
10

PEOPLE
1
2
3
4
5
6
7
8
9
10

CELEBS
1
2
3
4
5
6
7
8
9
10

POSSESSIONS
1
2
3
4
5
6
7
8
9
10

TUNES
1
2
3
4
5
6
7
8
9
10

DESIGNERS
1
2
3
4
5
6
7
8
9
10

MAGAZINES
1
2
3
4
5
6
7
8
9
10

ANIMALS
1
2
3
4
5
6
7
8
9
10

What's going on?

The things that that happen to you as you grow older can be super confusing. But fret not, it happens to everyone — you are NOT weird. And remember, whatever's going on in your life, you are unique and wonderful!

Love Ali xxx

Rollercoaster

Moody or what! Growing up can be a rough ride.
One minute you're on top of the world, the next,
you're down in the dumps.

So what's going on? It's the dreaded hormones, that's what!
Any time from the age of seven, a teeny gland at the base of
your brain sends hormones (which are chemicals) into your
bloodstream. When these hormones reach your ovaries, they
kick-start your ovaries into action. The ovaries start to produce
sex hormones, oestrogen and progesterone, and these will
trigger periods. Simple as that! It's all very clever, and pretty
crucial – after all, you may well want to have babies one day
way into the future!

And now the science bit

Every month a tiny egg cell ripens
in one of the ovaries and makes
its way to the uterus. The lining
in the uterus thickens to make a
soft bed for the egg in case it's
fertilized (the egg is fertilized
by having unprotected sex).
The unfertilized egg and the
lining break down and flow
slowly out of you body and
that's what a period is.

Moody The trouble is, it's not just your body that changes; your mood can be affected too. And although your body will settle down into a pattern, the mood swings can keep on coming with each period!

PMS The mood change a week or so before your period starts is known as PMS (pre-menstrual syndrome). Everyone is different, and you may not even notice much of a change. You may also find that once you actually get your period, you feel energetic and optimistic.

However things affect you, don't panic, because there are lots of ways you can make yourself feel good.

Action Stations

Some days nothing's right. You hate the way you look, you hate the way you feel and everything's just YUCK. Hormones do funny things during puberty. But don't let it get you down, there's lots you can do to lift your mood — here are some top tips!

Exercise

Play tennis

Go walking

Go swimming

Play football

Go dancing

Listen to music

Go cycling

These are all great ways to make you feel better!

Read a good book
BOOK
Eat healthily
Best
Friends
Have a laugh with a friend
Sleep well
Z z z Z

Moody Blues

If you get irritable, sad or over-sensitive before your period, it's a good idea to give yourself some warning. That way you can plan your month and give yourself (and everyone else!) a break on those bad days — and know that you're going to feel better again soon. You can also book yourself some special treats that are sure to help you through like seeing a movie, giving yourself a facial or a sleepover with friends.

Over the page is a fab mood chart for you to fill in. You'll be able to keep track of your state of mind, know the reason why you're being such a pain or feel like crying every two seconds. So turn over and get cracking. This is your chance to take control of your moods. Rule them instead of letting them rule you!

Mood Chart

DAY	MONTH 3: March	MO
1	premenstrual + irritable	●
2	X Achy + bit agitated	●
3	X I could kill my brother!	●
4	X Much happier	●
5	X ok— too much homework tho	●
	X Happy days!	●

X marks the spot!

Mark each day of your period with an X, colour code the dates when you feel great or grim, and scribble in just how you felt. Even if you haven't started your period yet, its worth filling in the chart you may notice a pattern in your moods...

DAY	MONTH 1:		MONTH 2:	
1	○		○	
2	○		○	
3	○		○	
4	○		○	
5	○		○	
6	○		○	
7	○		○	
8	○		○	
9	○		○	
10	○		○	
11	○		○	
12	○		○	
13	○		○	
14	○		○	

After filling in the chart for a
few months you may start to
see a definite pattern.
Experiment to see what
makes you feel better on
grotty days, whether it is
swimming, hanging out with
your mates or lying in bed
listening to music.
You're in charge – YOU
decide what's good for you.
Just don't be a victim to your
body! When you run out of
space here, use your regular
diary to track your moods.

17	○
18	○
19	○
20	○
21	○
22	○
23	○
24	○
25	○
26	○
27	○
28	○
29	○
30	○
31	○

KEY

GREEN Cool, anything goes

ORANGE Treat with caution –
could go either way

RED Danger – don't go there!

DAY	MONTH 3:	MONTH 4:	MONTH 5:	MONTH 6:
1	○	○	○	○
2	○	○	○	○
3	○	○	○	○
4	○	○	○	○
5	○	○	○	○
6	○	○	○	○
7	○	○	○	○
8	○	○	○	○
9	○	○	○	○
10	○	○	○	○
11	○	○	○	○
12	○	○	○	○
13	○	○	○	○
14	○	○	○	○

17
18
19
20
21
22
23
24
25
26
27
28
29
30
31

Repeat After Me

When you're feeling down, you may need a reminder of how totally fabulous, lovable and gorgeous you are. It's what YOU think of yourself that counts. After all, if YOU love you, everyone else will too! So, here goes . . .

I'm unique

I'm special

I'm
gorgeous

Recite as many
times a day
as you can, and
BELiEVE it!

I'm
lovable

I ♥ me!

More
good stuff
about me . . .

· · · · · · · · · · · · · · · · ·
· · · · · · · · · · · · · · · · ·

· · · · · · · · · · · · · · · ·
· · · · · · · · · · · ·

· · · · · · · · · · · · · · ·
· · · · · · · · · · ·

Mood-o-meter

Date	Mood-o-meter reading	What I did to feel better
6th June	Red alert	Had a yummy hot chocolate with whipped cream

On red alert days, avoid stressful situations, accept that you're not your normal cheery, positive self, and that you WILL feel better soon. Try not to argue with your parents, snap at your friends, or strangle your little brother. And don't give yourself a hard time either. You should be giving yourself a treat instead!

How bad did you feel on a scale of 1–10?	What was your score after taking action?
Before: 8 ½	After: 3
10 = v. bad	

RED ALERT!

Happy Collage

A collage is a brilliant way to put together pictures of lots of the things that make you feel peaceful, calm and happy, whether it's waves crashing onto the beach, a butterfly on a summer's day, a cute puppy, photos of your friends or a gorgeous dress in a magazine! You can turn to your collage when you need a reminder that life is worth living!

So get cutting
and sticking!

If you run out of space
here, make a bigger
'#aPPY COLLage'
and stick it on your
bedroom wall

What are you like?

Are you a tomboy or a girly girl? One of the best things about life is that you can choose what you want to be! We all like doing different things, that's what makes us who we are. What kind of person are you?

What would be your idea of a good time? Circle the number closest to the statement which applies most to you.

1 Having a make-up session 1 2 3 4 5 Having a pillow fight

2 Playing board games 1 2 3 4 5 Playing football

3 Making a dress 1 2 3 4 5 Making a mess

4 Watching a rom com 1 2 3 4 5 Watching a scary movie

5 Partying the night away 1 2 3 4 5 Camping under the stars

6 Going shopping 1 2 3 4 5 Going exploring

What you are like!

1–10 Girly-girl or what! You're unashamedly feminine, and just love being a girl. Enjoy it!

11–20 You're an in-betweener. Sometimes you feel like floating about in pink pjs, sometimes you're slobbing about in combat gear — it all depends on your mood!

21–30 You are definitely tomboy material! If you're not climbing trees, you're scoring a goal or off on some sort of adventure. Life is definitely not going to pass you by!

When things go wrong

It's easy to say 'be happy and confident' but it's not always easy to feel it. Things just don't work out that well sometimes. A tough home life, depression, lack of confidence and self-esteem, pressure to look like a stick-thin model — any of these things can lead to various problems, including eating disorders.

There is no way of knowing who will develop an eating disorder. Anorexia and Bulimia are complex psychological diseases and they can be hard to spot because sufferers are so secretive. But here are some signs to look out for:

Loss of weight
Excessive exercising
Constant excuses for missing meals
Obsession with food and calories
Going to the loo after eating
Wearing baggy clothes
Feeling cold
Moodiness

Anorexia Nervosa — dieting and obsessive exercising:
It's not about being thin, it's about being in control. It can quickly become very serious. Anorexics believe they are fat, no matter how skinny they are, and one in five die of starvation before they can be treated.

Bulimia Nervosa — bingeing on food and being sick:
Bulimics will deliberately overeat, then make themselves sick, or take laxatives. They have a bad self-image, and feel ashamed and anxious about their disorder.

Sufferers often don't recognize that they are ill. But they need help urgently, because both Anorexia and Bulimia are life-threatening illnesses. If you think you or one of your friends might have an eating disorder, speak to a trusted adult, or if you are too shy or embarrassed to do that, there are organisations that can help you:

Eating Disorders Association Youthline:
Tel: 0845 634 7650; text: 07786 201 820; email: fyp@b-eat.co.uk; website: www.b-eat.co.uk & www.edauk.com

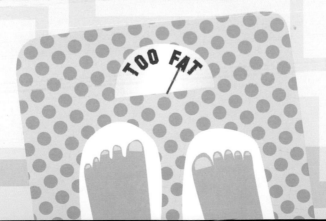

self

Everyone has bad days, even celebs, but don't let them get you down. Use my top tips on loving yourself and you'll be sure to banish those blues!

Love Ali xxx

Learn to love the skin you're in!

What do you see when you look in the mirror?
Do you sometimes love yourself, sometimes hate yourself?
Nothing new there, then! The thing is, life is a lot more fun
if you can learn to love yourself,
so have a go at this:

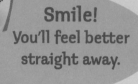

Smile!
You'll feel better
straight away.

Don't obsess
about weight –
thinner is not
better!

Accept the way you
look – that's the way
you're supposed to be.

Focus on something you DO like about yourself and keep it in your mind.

Tell yourself you are unique, gorgeous, there's no one quite like you.

2 1 3

REMEMBER REMEMBER AND NEVER FORGET that pictures of girls and women in magazines are airbrushed!

Before

MAGAZINE

After

They all have pimples, dimples and wobbly bits in real life. Plus they spend a whole HEAP of time, energy and money on looking good, because that's their job! Your job is to enjoy your life, enjoy your friends and family, and focus on yourself as a person.

Half empty or half full ?

See how you score in the half-empty half-full test?

Does only good stuff happen to positive people or is it just that they refuse to see the bad side of things? Whatever it is, life is much more fun if you allow it to be!

1 You want to learn to skateboard. Do you:
a) Think it's much too hard and you'll never be able to do it?
b) Get your shin pads, grit your teeth and hope for the best?

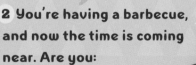

2 You're having a barbecue, and now the time is coming near. Are you:
a) Sure it's going to rain, the food won't cook, no one will turn up and it'll be a disaster?
b) Happy your friends are coming, and know it'll be fun whatever the weather?

3 **You like the look of a boy at school. Do you:**

a) Ignore it, there's no way he's going to be interested in you?

b) Decide to talk to him , it's worth getting to know him, and maybe you'll get on?

4 **You would love to audition for the school play. Do you:**

a) Decide there's no point, you'll never get a part

b) Go for it anyway — you'd like to be involved, even if you only play a tree!

5 **You've seen a hairstyle you like in a magazine. Do you:**

a) Think you'll never look as good as the model so you may as well forget it?

b) Book an appointment, take the pic with you and tell the hairdresser to get cracking?

Mostly As

Wow, you're treating life like one big chore. Don't be on such a downer — pessimism isn't the way forward. Try to get out of the negative frame of mind, believe in yourself and give things a go — what's the worst that can happen?

Mostly Bs

Way to go! You are a classic optimist. Your dreams may not fall into your lap just like that but you're going to give life your best shot!

Bad to Good in Five Easy Steps!

You only have one life, so enjoy it! Turn negative to positive, and remember that good things can happen just as easily as bad.

1 Look on any problem as a challenge, a chance to prove yourself

2 Treat life as one big opportunity. Don't miss out on anything

3 If something's hard, try it anyway. Stop moaning and get cracking!

4 Don't waste your energy worrying about the small stuff. Go for gold!

5 Take that frown off your face and

SMILE SMILE SMILE!

How to say no!

You must never do anything that makes you feel uncomfortable — why should you? If you don't agree with something, or are being pressured in any way, you need to say no, and mean it.

Top tips for saying NO:

★ Don't get angry — count to ten!

★ Be strong and walk away

★ Agree to disagree

★ Talk it through and explain how you feel

★ Stick to your guns

Pat Yourself on the Back

How often do you focus on the things you achieve, however small? Sometimes the things that go wrong take up much more braintime than the things that go right — and you might not even realize what a total star you are.

Make a list of everything positive you do, from smiling at the grumpy lady next door, helping your mum make dinner, giving your best friend a gorgeous birthday present to picking out the best T-shirt in the shop. It won't take long before you run out of room. Then you really will feel good about yourself!

. . . .

. . . .

. . . .

. . . .

. . . .

. . . .

. . . .

. . . .

. . . .

. . . .

. . . .

. . . .

The Golden Rules for a Happy Life

Be positive

Never give up

Speak up if you think something's wrong

Don't compare yourself to others

Do things your way

Stand up for yourself

Never be afraid
to say NO

Stick to
your guns

Hang on to your dreams

Turn problems
into challenges

LOVE
YOURSELF!

Believe in
yourself

Trust your instincts

Stay in
control

Dear Me . . .

Feeling angry, sad, frustrated, confused or worried, but not ready to share it with anyone? Just write it down. Emotions run wild in your head if you let them, and problems can seem much worse than they actually are.

Create your own problem page, and try to work out what you can do to feel better. Don't forget that every problem has a solution. You might need help to deal with it, but there will be an answer. And remember that you are not alone — whatever problem you are facing, someone else will be facing it too!

SAMPLE LETTER

Dear Me,

It really annoys me when my brother just barges into my bedroom. I never get any privacy in this house!

Love Me

x

Solutions:

* Put ~~KEEP OUT~~ notice on door (he'd probably ignore it)
* Get a lock (if Mum and Dad let me)
* Barge into his room (so he knows how it feels)
* Talk to him (if he'll listen)
* Talk to parents (I'll make them listen)

Healthy Body, Healthy Mind

Eating well, exercising and getting enough sleep — these three things will help keep you feeling (and looking) good.

Eat:

★ Loads of fruit and veg – at least five portions every day
★ Lots of bread, potatoes, rice, pasta, cereals
★ Some meat, fish, eggs, beans or lentils
★ A bit of milk, cheese, yoghurt
★ Biscuits, chocolate and sweets – occasionally, for a special treat!

* Junk food makes you sluggish — try not to have too much of it.

Exercise

It is good for your brain as well as your body. It gives you energy, makes you happy and helps you sleep — what more could you want?

Sleep

Your body is working hard with all these changes you're going through. It repairs itself while you sleep, so give it nine to ten hours rest every night!

Sleep Talking!

Do you sleep curled up like a baby or splayed out like a star?

The position you sleep in can reveal your personality!

**STARFISH POSITION —
splayed out like a star**
You like to help others,
and you hate to be the
centre of attention.

BABY POSITION — curled up tight
You're tough on the outside, but a big softy inside.

LOG POSITION — lying on your side with arms by your side
You're easy-going, sociable and good with new people, but you can be gullible.

ZOMBIE POSITION — lying on your side with arms out in front
You seem to be easy-going but you're a very careful character. You like to know all the facts before you make a decision.

SOLDIER POSITION — lying on your back, arms by your side and legs slightly apart
You're quite reserved and hate fuss. You expect a lot of yourself and others.

FREEFALLER POSITION — lying on your front, arms either side of your head
You're optimistic and outgoing but also practical and down-to-earth. You don't take criticism well.

Recognize yourself? If you don't know how you sleep, you'll have to get a mate to take a photo of you! If you toss and turn all night, it means you're a mixture of all these types — how confusing!

Sweet Dreams

The average person has 1,460 dreams per year — That's over four a night! Your dreams can help you make sense of things happening in your waking life.

Here are some common 'worry' dreams and what they might mean . . .

You're being chased, but you don't know why, or who is chasing you

You're way too busy and feel like you're on the run – slow down!

You're looking for something. You keep on and on searching but can't find it

There's something in your life you need to sort out

You need to make a phone call, but the buttons don't work, you dial the wrong number and the person can't hear you

You need to get something off your chest

You're about to take a test at school but realize you have missed all the lessons, and there's no way you can pass it

You have too many things on your plate!

You're out shopping when you suddenly realize you're naked! But nobody else notices

A new experience is making you anxious but nobody else knows

Dream Catcher

Keep a note of the dreams you remember.
Especially the recurring ones. If you write them down,
you might even be able to make sense of them.

Write your
dreams in the
bubbles

Friend or Foe?

What are you scared of? Spiders? Snakes?

Check these out . . .

There are lots of strange phobias around and there are lots of strange names for them too. There's even a name for being scared of school!

Ablutophobia
Fear of washing

Arachnophobia
Fear of spiders

Arachibutyrophobia
Fear of peanut butter sticking to the roof of the mouth!

13

Triskaidekaphobia
Fear of the number 13!

Scolionophobia
Fear of school

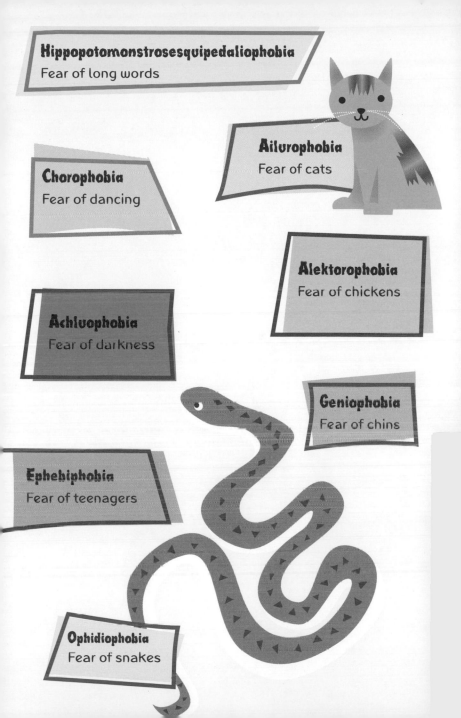

Hippopotomonstrosesquipedaliophobia
Fear of long words

Ailurophobia
Fear of cats

Chorophobia
Fear of dancing

Alektorophobia
Fear of chickens

Achluophobia
Fear of darkness

Geniophobia
Fear of chins

Ephebiphobia
Fear of teenagers

Ophidiophobia
Fear of snakes

Love your Life

No-one's life is
perfect but if you
think positive,
be yourself and
love your life, you
can make it pretty
darned fabulous.

Love Ali xxx

Making friends — and keeping them!

Friends are what life is all about. No one can do without them! Follow these top tips and you'll have friends for life.

Making friends is easy . . .

Ask questions — and listen to the answers

Tell a joke (but only if it's funny!)

Smile and look happy and friendly

Pay a compliment (but don't overdo it!)

Take up a new sport!

Organize a sleepover

Be yourself, and act natural

Join an after-school club club

Keeping them is harder . . .

★ Keep other people's secrets secret ★ Keep promises
★ Stay loyal ★ Be a friend through good and bad times
★ Treat friends the way you'd like to be treated
★ Don't dump old mates for the sake of new ones
★ Introduce them to each other
★ Don't dump old mates for a boyfriend ★ Don't forget them

Good mates . . .

DO Listen ★ Include you ★ Stick up for you
★ Support you ★ Consider your feelings
DON'T Exclude you ★ Gossip about you ★ Feel jealous of you
★ Make you feel bad ★ Expect you to spend all your
time with them

Be Yourself!

Your friends love you because you're you!
But how true to yourself are you? Find out in this fab quiz!

1. Your friends are rude about a girl you like.
Do you:
   a) Say nothing?
   b) Say she's OK, and tell your friends
   they're being mean?
   c) Agree with your friends and join in?

2. One of your friends gets jealous when you go shopping with
another mate. Do you:
   a) Tell your jealous mate she's got a problem and needs to sort it out?
   b) Arrange to go shopping next time with the jealous mate?
   c) Tell your jealous friend you'll never go shopping without her again?

3. A friend keeps asking you where you buy your
clothes, and then turns up wearing the same gear
as you! Do you:
   a) Start lying about where you go shopping?
   b) Take it as a compliment?
   c) Go shopping with her and suggest different
   clothes that would look good on her?

4. A friend has a horrible haircut. Do you:
a) Lie and say you love it?
b) Tell her it suits her?
c) Tell her that her hair will grow back soon?

5. A friend invites you to go on holiday with her, but you really don't like her brother because he teases you all the time. Do you:

a) Say thanks but no thanks?
b) Tell her you're busy that week?
c) Say you'd love to, but explain that you have a problem with her brother?

6. You realize that a mate has been copying your work in class. Do you:

a) Hide your work from now on?
b) Ask your teacher if you can sit somewhere else?
c) Tell your friend to stop cheating and do her own work!?

	a	b	c
1	2	3	1
2	3	2	1
3	3	1	2
4	3	1	2
5	2	1	3
6	1	2	3

If you scored 6–10 points:
Speak your mind, girl!
It's good that you're considerate of others' feelings but not at your own expense.
Sometimes you need to look after number one, and say what you really think.
Be brave! It may not feel right, but in the long run, your friends will respect you for it.

If you scored 11–14 points:
You've got it just sussed!
You seem to have a perfect balance. You're not afraid to say what you really
think, but you're careful not to hurt others' feelings. Good job!

If you scored 15 points or more:
Too much/Calm down!
Easy, tiger! You're one confident lady! Well done for saying what you really think,
but make sure you don't upset anyone. Sometimes the truth can be hurtful,
so just be careful.

YOU time – becaus

It's great to hang out with friends and family and to be super sociable, but it's also important to slow down sometimes, and enjoy time on your own.

CHiLL OUT!

So, turn off your mobile, run a bubble bath, fetch the chocolate, grab a magazine and relax! Then get into your PJs and cuddle up with your favourite cushion and watch your best ever DVD. Simple!

you're worth it

BUSY BEE!
If you'd rather have a busy YOU time, why not sort out your photo album, finish making that friendship bracelet, try on all your clothes, re-arrange your bedroom — anything that grabs you. Just enjoy being YOU!

The Troubl

Do your parents drive you crazy?
Sometimes they just don't get it!
How painful are your parents?!

Tick the box if they:

1 Tell your mates stories about when you were small

2 Dance in public

3 Use uncool expressions

4 Say things were better when they were young

5 Ask you to turn your music down

6 Make you tidy your room

7 Ask stupid questions at parents' evenings

8 Call you 'young lady' when they're cross with you

9 Say: 'Because I say so'; 'When I was your age . . .';
' It's just a phase'; 'You'll find out when you're older'

10 Tell you things you already know

11 Tell you off in front of your friends

12 Ruffle your hair lovingly!

with Parents

cha
cha
cha

twist
twist

What makes your parents tick?
- Under 5 ticks: your parents are seriously cool – lucky you!
- 5–10 ticks: sometimes they're a bit dodgy, but on the whole, they're liveable with
- Over 10 ticks: poor thing. Your parents need serious training. Get on to it!

Now turn over for 'The Good Thing about Parents'!

The Good Thing about Parents

OK, so they can be totally embarrassing and majorly annoying, but there are good things about parents too!

★ Always there for you

★ Never forget your birthday

★ Cook your fave meals

★ Look after you when you're ill

★ Hug you when you're sad

★ Take you on holiday

★ Love you for ever, no matter what

My parents are special because

. . . .
. . . .
. . . .
. . . .

Boys — Yuck or Yum?

You may be just too busy enjoying life with your mates to give boys a look-in. But if there's a cutey you can't stop thinking about, before you go any further, there are a lot of 'Don'ts' to deal with!

Don't let him make you doubt how lovely you are

Don't spend all your time with him

Don't put up with rubbish behaviour — why should you?

Don't let any boy break your heart!

Don't drop your mates

Don't go thinking everything he says is right

Don't go out with a jealous boy — he'll want you to drop all your mates and he'll start to control your life

Don't think any boy is perfect — he's no more perfect than you are!

Don't try and hang on to a boy at all costs — if he likes you, you won't need to — he'll be hanging on to you for dear life!

Don't ever let a boy pressure you into anything

Don't dream of thinking your life isn't worth living without him

Don't let him become the centre of your universe — make him an added extra

Don't think there is something wrong with you if you don't have a boyfriend or don't want one

Don't change — be yourself

If you can handle all these 'Don'ts', then go ahead and get to know that cutey! Just never forget that you are gorgeous and any boy should feel honoured if you're even the slightest bit interested in him!

Pot-luck PJ Party

Duvets, DVDs, PJs and pigging out with your friends. It's so cool! The pot-luck part is simple — everyone brings a surprise something to eat.
Check out these perfect pot luck PJ party recipes:

One cool Strawberry Smoothie:

1 cup of strawberries
1 cup of plain yogurt
Clear honey

* Blend the strawberries until finely crushed
* Mix in the yoghurt
* Sweeten with honey, pour into a glass — sorted!

Warm Chocolate Bananas and Ice Cream:

Bananas – however many you fancy
Chocolate buttons
Tin foil
Vanilla ice cream

* Leaving skin on, make little cuts through the banana with a knife
* Push the chocolate buttons in as far as you can
* Wrap in foil, bake in warm oven (180°C) for about 40 minutes until soft and squishy!
* Eat with ice cream – yum!
* Be careful, they'll be HOT!

Broken Biscuit Cake:

100g butter
3 tablespoons golden syrup
3 tablespoons cocoa
2 teaspoons lemon juice
200g roughly broken biscuits

* Melt butter, syrup and cocoa in a pan over a low heat
* Add the lemon juice
* Stir the biscuits in well
* Turn into a buttered flan dish and press down with the back of a spoon
* Leave to cool in fridge, and hey presto!

Having a Laugh

Laughing is really important! It lowers stress and is good for the immune system too. Six-year-olds laugh about 300 times a day, but poor old stressy adults only laugh between 15 and 100 times . . .

If you hear a good joke, write it down – you never know when it will come in handy! Short ones are the best and easiest to memorize.

....
....
....
....
....
....

....
....
....
....
....
....

Most Embarrassing Moments

Ever fallen flat on your face, called your teacher Mum, or forgotten your lines in the school play? You can be sure that anything that makes you die of embarrassment at the time will make you die laughing later on! Store up those treasured memories and score them on the cringe-o-meter.

CRINGE-O-METER

= blush-worthy

! = red from big toe to eyebrows

!! = head-in-hands awful

!!! = this CANNOT be happening to me

!!!! = please swallow me up and let me disappear off the face of the earth

What, Why, When?

Every single person is different, so it's totally tricksy to include everything that might happen to all of you. But lots of the same things will come up, so here are some top tips. And remember, LOVE YOURSELF — ALWAYS!

Love Ali xxx

Feeling Mad, Sad, Bad?

Q Sometimes I just feel sad for no reason at all. What's going on?

A It's those hormones again! They're zooming around and getting you all upset. Don't worry, things will settle down. Meanwhile, try hugging the dog, stroking the cat, singing along to your favourite track, treating yourself to your favourite snack!

Q I dread getting my period because it makes me feel really quiet and weird, and I just sort of turn in on myself. Help!

A Accept that you're going to get times like this, and try to make the most of them. Why not save up lots of nice things to do on those days when you're not quite yourself — a really good book, your favourite magazine, that DVD you've been wanting to see for ages. Then at least those dodgy days will have a silver lining!

Q I'm not sure if I'm depressed or just fed up in a 'normal' way. How do you know the difference?

A Depression is an illness caused by a chemical or hormonal imbalance. The symptoms include loss of appetite, lack of concentration, lack of energy, feelings of hopelessness and extreme sadness. It can also stop you from sleeping. If you think you're suffering from depression, you need to get help, just as you would for a physical illness — you can't just 'snap out of it'. The important thing is not to be ashamed of how you're feeling.

Q What exactly is PMS?

A PMS stands for 'pre-menstrual syndrome' — it's the combination of symptoms that some girls suffer from a week or so before their period. As well as affecting the body, PMS affects the brain, causing mood swings. You may feel sad, irritable or anxious. Once your period comes, you should be back to your normal cheery self!

Losing Your Cool

Q **I get embarrassed really easily and can't stop blushing. Help!**

A When you're little, you're not self-conscious and you just get on with your life. As you get older, you become more aware of yourself as an individual, and you start to worry about what sort of impression you're making, and how other people are reacting to you. Try not to let it get to you – as your confidence grows, the blushing will gradually get under control until you won't even realize you haven't had red cheeks for weeks! Remember, it happens to everyone – even the most confident people.

Q **I want to audition for the school play, but I'm really nervous!**

A Why not just offer to help back-stage? That way you can be involved but not be in the spot-light – and maybe next time you can go for an acting part.

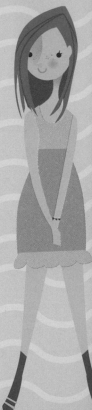

Q **I get teased for being flat-chested and it's really getting me down.**

A It's hard being teased, but try to remember that the size of your breasts is not the most important thing about you! Focus on what is important, like the fact that you're funny, and a lovely person, a whiz at maths, an ace guitarist, a well-good swimmer – I bet the list is endless!

Q My big sister is so cool. I wish I could be more like her.

A The coolest thing is to not care about being cool. Don't try to be something you're not; don't compare yourself to anyone else. Just be yourself.

Q I always leave my homework till the last minute. I know I have to do it, but I just can't get started. Then I get in a real panic and don't have time to do all of it.

A The trick to getting anything done is to break it down into little chunks, so it doesn't feel like such a big deal. Give yourself a treat after completing each bit, whether it's phoning a mate, eating something nice, watching a TV programme (just the one!), or going on a bike ride. Before you know it, the whole job will be done!

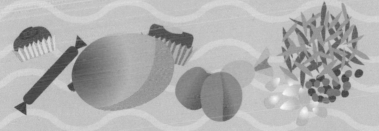

Problem Parents!

Q My mum re-married and now I have a step-dad. He's OK, but he keeps telling me what to do. He's not my real dad, and I don't see why I should listen to him.

A It's always difficult to adjust to a new situation. Try explaining how you feel to your mum. Your step-dad is probably trying to sort out how to deal with your new situation too. Give it time – and see how it goes.

Q My parents are so annoying. They treat me like I'm about four years old!

A As you grow older, you feel like a separate person to your family, and you want to be more and more independent. But it's hard for your parents to accept that you're not their 'little girl' any more. It's an in-between stage, and everyone just needs time to get used to it. The more you show your mum and dad how grown-up and responsible you can be, the more they'll start treating you as you'd like to be treated.

Q My mother is ruining my life! She won't let me do anything!

A Ask yourself why your mother won't let you do stuff. And what is it exactly that she won't let you do? Does she let you wear what you like? See the friends you like? Decide what's really important to you, and what you can live without? Tell her how you'd use your new independence – keep her involved and she'll learn to trust you more and more.

Q **My dad doesn't want me to wear make-up. He's so old-fashioned.**

A When it comes to their little girls, dads can be funny about things like make-up or clothes. Explain that you just want to start experimenting. Don't slap it on with a paint brush – be subtle about it, and he'll gradually get used to the idea that his daughter is growing up.

Q **All my friends get an allowance from their parents. My mum buys me stuff, but that means she's always in charge of what I'm getting.**

A Tell your mum you'd like to learn to look after money yourself. It's good practice for the future, after all. Perhaps you could suggest earning extra money by doing some chores around the house? When you have some money saved up, why don't you suggest going shopping with your mum? That way she won't feel left out – but make sure you show her the stuff YOU like – you're buying it after all!

Friends for life?

Q Some of my friends are really outgoing and funny and it makes me feel so boring.

A Your friends obviously like you, so I wouldn't worry. There's room for quiet people in this world too, you know. Imagine if we were all scrabbling to be the centre of attention.

Q My best friend wants me to lie to my parents so we can go out. I don't want to.

A She's not much of a friend then! No one should make you do anything you're not happy with. Just say no – she'll respect you for it, even if she's fed up at first. If you say yes against your will, you won't feel right.

Q I love my friends, but sometimes I just want to be on my own. They think I'm being stand-offish, but I'm not.

A Everyone needs 'me' time. Schedule in some time with your friends, and explain that sometimes you need time to be alone. Real friends will understand that.

Q My friend's parents are divorcing and she's really upset. I don't know what to say or do to help her.

A Sounds like you are doing what your friend needs most at the moment – being a good mate! Be there for her and let her talk about it – even if that's all she can talk about. Be a shoulder to cry on. She'll get through it, with friends like you around.

Q My best mate is driving me crazy. When I get new clothes, she buys the same ones, and now she's got the same haircut as me. At this rate, she's not going to be my mate for much longer!

A She admires your style, and hasn't yet got the confidence to experiment with her own. Why not go shopping with her, and try to show her other stuff that looks good on her. She'll be much happier doing her own thing in the end.

Boy Talk

Q My best friend is nuts about this boy at school. She wants us to double-date, but I'm just not interested — I'd much rather hang out with my girlfriends. Am I normal?

A Of course you're normal! Everyone's different. The best thing is knowing what you want, and not getting drawn into an uncomfortable situation. Why not suggest a few of you get together — that way you won't feel like you're on a date, and you won't be letting your friend down either.

Q I've been dumped by my boyfriend. I don't think I'll ever be happy again.

A Well if that were true, there'd be a lot of unhappy people around! We've all been dumped some time or other. Don't mope too much, get out and about with your mates. That boy wasn't the only fish in the sea — there's another one just around the corner . . .

Q My boyfriend is really sweet when we're on our own, but when he's with his mates, he's like a different person!

A Most people change when they're in a crowd. Your boyfriend doesn't want to appear 'soft' when he's with his mates — he reserves that for you! Let him spend time with his mates without you — and enjoy the boy he is when you're alone together.

Q I don't think I'm ever going to get a boyfriend. I'm just not the kind of girl boys go for.

A There's no specific type of girl who boys go for. Some girls might be a bit more flirty, confident and upfront about it all, but it doesn't mean a boy is going to be interested! Why not join a club or take up a sport? That way you'll meet like-minded boys (and girls!), and you can take your time to get to know a boy properly. Going on a date will be a natural step!

Q I sometimes get really jealous when my friends joke around with my boyfriend. It wells up inside me till I feel like I'm going to explode.

A Jealousy brings nothing but trouble. It's a totally negative feeling that eats you up, and it just keeps making you feel worse and worse. Try to work out why you're feeling this way — you should be happy your friends like your boyfriend. And he's with you, not them, isn't he?

nobody likes a bully . . .

Q There's a new girl at my school, and my group of friends are being really horrible to her. I don't like it, but I don't want to lose my friends. What shall I do?

A Well firstly, don't join in just to keep in with your friends. Perhaps you could talk to them one by one and tell them how you feel about it. If they don't listen, you need to ask yourself if they're the kind of friends you want. Bullying isn't acceptable under any circumstances.

Q There's a group of boys at school who call me names and make me feel really bad. What can I do about it?

A Tell someone straight away. Talk to a teacher, a friend, your parents, or someone you trust. And remember that although you've asked for their help, you don't have to let them take over. You can work through it with them, and discuss what you would like to happen.

Q I've started hanging out with a group of girls from school at the weekends but they're ignoring my best mate and won't let her hang around with us. What shall I do?

A They can't be that cool if they're behaving like this. Stand up for your mate. If you don't, you're as bad as these girls and you're a bully too.

Q Why do bullies bully?

A There are lots of reasons why someone might bully: they may have problems at home; they may be getting bullied themselves; they may feel that they don't fit in, and are bullying before they get bullied. They may want to show off and seem tough. They most likely don't like themselves very much, so they're taking it out on someone else. They need help as much as the person they are bullying.

Lifelines

If you don't feel able to talk to anyone you know, don't fret, there are other options. Here is a selection of useful and informative website and helplines:

General help and advice:

• NSPCC: Tel: 0808 0800 5000;
website: www.nspcc.org.uk
• Childline: Tel: 0800 1111;
website: www.childline.org.uk
• Youth Access Helpline: Tel: 0208 772 9900;
open Monday-Friday between 9am and 1pm and 2pm and 5pm

- www.youngminds.org.uk
- Samaritans: Tel: 08457 909 090;
website: www.samaritans.org.uk;
email: jo@samaritans.org.uk
- www.beinggirl.co.uk
- BBC Onion Street: website: www.bbc.co.uk/
schools/communities/onionstreet

Bullying:

- www.bullying.co.uk
- www.kidscape.org.uk
- www.childline.org.uk/bullying.asp
- www.anti-bullyingalliance.org

Eating Disorders:

- Eating Disorders
Association Youthline:
Tel: 0845 634 7650;
text: 07786 201 820;
email: fyp@b-eat.co.uk;
website: www.b-eat.co.uk
& www.edauk.com

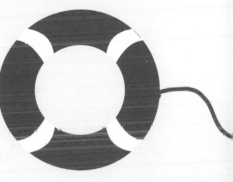

Glossary

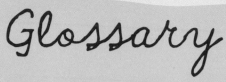

Contraception – the deliberate prevention of the conception of a baby, also called birth control. Lots of different methods are used, including condoms and the contraceptive pill

Eating Disorder – any of various disorders, such as anorexia nervosa or bulimia, that involve major disturbances in eating habits

Psychological – to do with the mind

Gland – a cell or organ that makes chemicals and gives them out into the body

Hormones – chemicals made in your brain that influence development of your body and mind when you reach puberty

Immune system – the parts of your body that protect you from getting sick

Oestrogen – a female hormone that causes development and change in the reproductive organs

Ovaries – the part of a girl's reproductive system where eggs (or ova) are made and stored

Progesterone – a female sex hormone which causes the uterus (womb) to prepare for pregnancy

Puberty – the time where your body changes from a child's body to that of an adult

Reproductive organs – the parts of the body involved in reproduction or having babies

Self-esteem – a realistic respect for or good impression of yourself

Sexual intercourse – the act of having sex

Stress – emotional or physical strain or tension

Unprotected sex – sexual intercourse without using contraception

Uterus – also called the womb. This is where babies grow from fertilized eggs until they are ready to be born. The uterus lining is shed every time you have a period

notes

Thoughts

. . . .

. . . .

. . . .

. . . .

. . . .

. . . .

. . . .

. . . .

Scribbles & Doodles

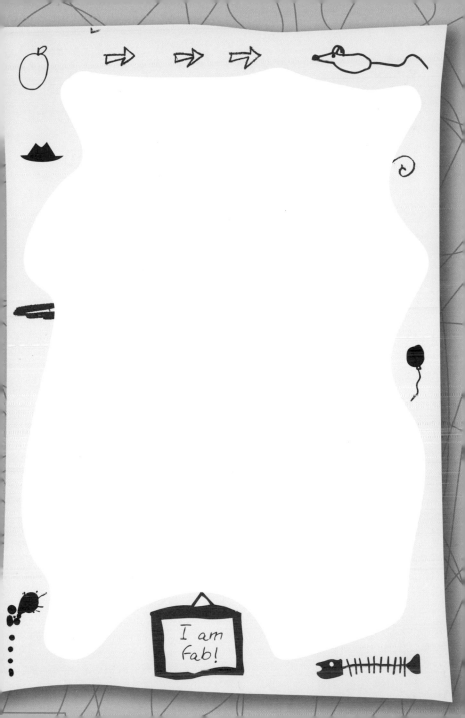

I am
Fab!

Secrets

....
....
....
....
....
....
....
....
....
....
....
....
....
....
....
....

The Secret Me

COMING SOON . . .

My Body

Ali Ritchie

If you feel like your body has a mind of its own and you don't understand what's happening to you, then this is the book for you. Find out what's going on and why, and that you are SO normal.